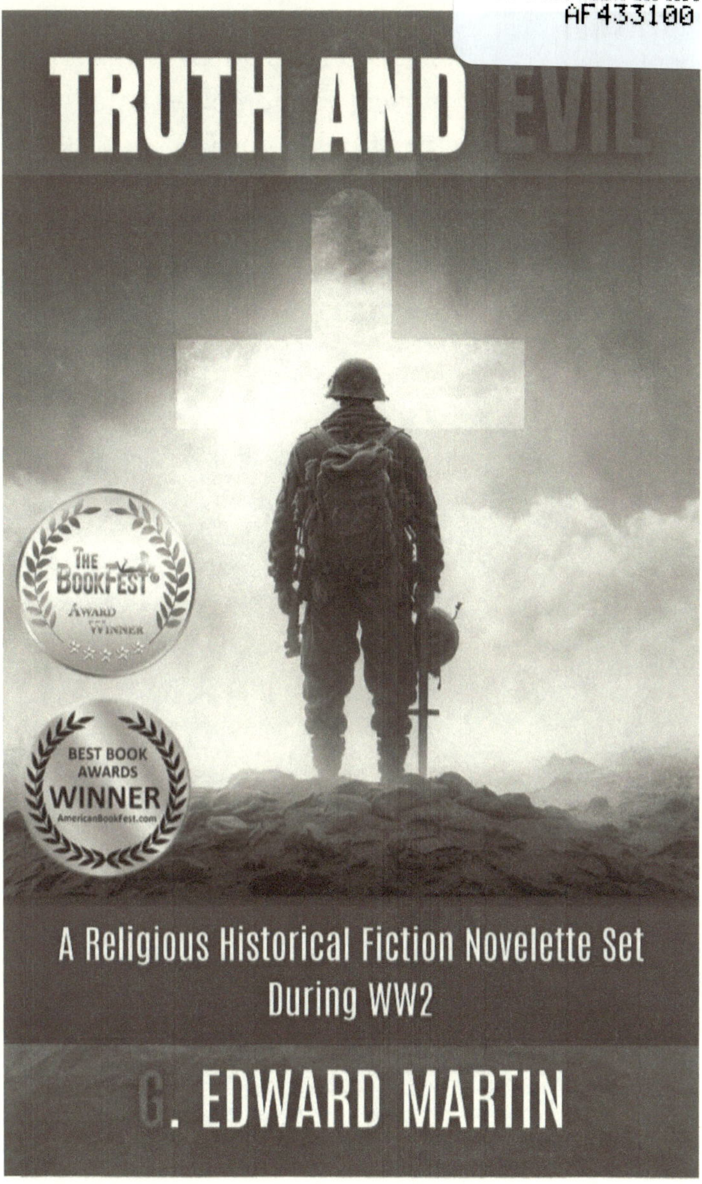
TRUTH AND EVIL
THE BOOKFEST® AWARD WINNER
BEST BOOK AWARDS WINNER AmericanBookFest.com
A Religious Historical Fiction Novelette Set During WW2
G. EDWARD MARTIN

Truth and Evil
A Christian Historical Fiction Novelette Set During World War II

Written by
G. Edward Martin

*****

Edited by
Christopher J. Agrella

*****

With contributions from
Carla P. Letellier and Dahlia Fazioli

Copyright 2024
G. Edward Martin
All Rights Reserved

WINNER: The BookFest, Fall 2024

Category: Christian, Historical

*****

WINNER: 2024 American Book Fest
Best Book Awards

Category: Fiction Novelette

*****

FINNALIST: 2024 American Book Fest
Best Book awards

Category: Religious Fiction

At the conclusion of this book, if you enjoyed this story, please consider leaving an honest review for this title on Amazon.com

Thank you for supporting indie authors!

A Warning from the Author

*****

This is the most difficult story I have written. It is difficult to read, and it was difficult to create. This story is intended *only* for adults.

This story confronts the very worst of humanity, as well as the very best. As you read this, there will undoubtedly be moments where you want to close it and walk away permanently. However, I promise that if you push through to the end, this story will reward you for it. I regard this as my greatest and most important work.

*****

The following story takes place during World War 2, but I could have easily written it within the context of several horrible events and wars of the twentieth century.

I have written this story to reiterate and re-explore the complex lessons which we need to glean from the last one hundred years. I fear that we have not learned those lessons, and thus, we are equally vulnerable to falling into the same mass-pathologies. For this reason, I am deeply troubled that this century may become a mirror image of the last. I fear we may be doomed to relearn that which we ought to already know.

In our ignorance, we believe ourselves to be more advanced and wiser than people who lived one hundred years ago. This is a foolish assumption. One hundred years is no time at all, and we refuse to have honest conversations about our own vulnerabilities.

Furthermore, as religion continues to fade from the consciousness of modern man, our morality will find itself standing upon a steadily shrinking island where it struggles to keep its feet firmly planted. I believe that people instinctually worship (whether we recognize it or not) and we put everything at risk when we remove God from His throne to be replaced by our leaders, celebrities, greed, ideologies, et cetera.

Even in modern times, with a few notable events of the last several years, I see clearly that our society is alarmingly vulnerable to slipping into states of mass psychosis and not recognizing this slow descent into the pit of Hell as we are rolling down to it.

With all these reasons in mind, I hope that this story can be my contribution to help prevent us from suffering such a fate. The only effective medicine to stave off such evils and ignorance is for each of us to fully know ourselves, and to speak the truth.

Thank you for being a reader, and I am grateful for your time.

-G. Edward Martin

Truth and Evil

*****

This is the story of a young German soldier's walk through a hell of his own making, on his journey back to heaven.

*****

There was once a young German soldier in the year 1942. He was twenty years old and had been drafted into the army two years earlier.

Before the war, he was just a simple boy from the countryside, living on his family's farm outside of Paderborn in Westphalia, obedient to his father and living a quiet life. He was a typical young man from Germany in that he had a decent education and a strong work ethic. He was neither good nor evil; he was just a boy moving into manhood and learning about the world.

Before the war, he loved to work on cars and joke with his childhood friends. He was terrified to speak to any attractive girl, and he played sports with the other boys from neighboring farms. Before the war, he had no idea what was within him or how big the world is. If he had been asked about his future, he would have looked around and shrugged, assuming his destiny was to farm like his own father and his father's father before him. However, when he joined the war, he soon met sides of himself that were patiently waiting behind closed doors for the right context to be unlocked.

Before he was drafted and during his service, the young soldier loved his country, and he never questioned the war. Two years earlier when he left his home, he readily accepted his call to service—considering it his sacred duty as a man and a son of Germany.

Now, after two years in the service of his country, he was no longer a simple farm boy. That simple child was a distant memory.

He had been in multiple fierce battles, and he had seen many things. There were times when he held fellow soldiers in his arms as they died. There were many times when he saw men bleed out and lose limbs, and sometimes, he was the cause of that agony, having been the man who pulled the trigger or threw the grenade.

Although he saw much death, he was never so much as scratched by a bullet or shrapnel. Because of this, a place deep within him felt that he was somehow chosen or protected, and he moved about the war with a sense of invincibility—believing that he was protected as a righteous man fighting a righteous war.

Fate was on his side as he worked to eradicate the enemy, and he had an unshakable belief that fate wanted the enemy eradicated.

The enemy, although resembling people, were not people in his mind. Whether they were Jewish, Gypsy, African, Polish, Russian or any *other*; they were not human. They were a plague, a curse upon the Earth. They were the diseased and rotting wood upon the forest floor, slowing the growth of mighty trees and needing to be purified by fire. This is what he was told, and this is what he believed. Alongside millions of other men and women who believed the same, this was his world view, taught to him from a young age.

In the spring of 1942, after two years of hard fighting in the service of his fatherland, he found himself in Soviet territory, going from town to town as part of a massive campaign to invade and defeat the USSR. The German army called this mission "Operation Barbarossa," and it had begun on a Sunday in late June of 1941, some nine months earlier.

It was an ambitious campaign, one which other conquerors such as Napoleon Bonaparte had once tried. None before had succeeded in conquering the vast Russian landscape, but the young soldier firmly believed this time would be different. This was the modern German army, the most powerful war machine to ever exist. The world had never seen a force like it—enormous, disciplined, determined, and composed of free men who were well-armed and technologically superior to any nation who had come before.

There was no country on Earth that could stand against this force, and the Germans knew it. Their army took as it pleased as it marched through Europe—swallowing up everything in its path, without any other country being able to even slow it down.

One warm day, the young soldier's platoon was clearing a small town, and he was standing in front of a house in a once quiet neighborhood as he awaited his next orders. The air was gray and foggy with the soot from the burning structures caused by aerial bombs, and the sun could only be guessed at through the thick, hazy cloud of smoke that enmeshed the air from ground to sky. The air was so thick with the soot that he could no longer even smell it, but it made his nose run and he sneezed as he stared at the empty houses.

He removed a handkerchief from his pocket to wipe his forehead and dripping nose, removing his heavy Stahlhelm helmet at the same time, seeking a moment of relief. It was a handkerchief his mother had given him many years back, and she had cut it herself from the original thin swaddle blanket he was first wrapped in on the day he was born.

Over the years, she had worked diligently to preserve the piece of thin cloth—lovingly washing it by hand and periodically mending the frayed edges. On the day he was packing to leave for the war, she handed this small corner of it to him, freshly removed from the drying line, and it went into his pocket that day, perfectly clean and bright.

Taking it out now, it was gray and black and smelled of gunpowder and sweat. He cleared his nose into it, and looked down as he slowly opened it. The fluid was dark, dull, and clotted with small bits of ash that had collected deep in his nostrils.

"Die Eingeascherten," or, "The Cremated," the young soldier and his platoon called this gray and black mixture of ashes and snot—joking that it was made from what was left of the Russians after the planes dropped bombs and immolated their bodies, scattering their ashes into the wind.

As he looked up from the handkerchief and observed the town, less than half the houses remained. The others had been leveled by airplanes, mortar shells, and resulting fires. For the structures still standing, the German soldiers were going door-to-door looking for people, food, and supplies. When they were satisfied that each town was searched and stripped, they often finished the job by burning down a few old structures and leaving others to be occupied by future German citizens once the Soviet Union had been conquered and subdued.

This town, like many in the Soviet Union, was poor and generally devoid of anything useful except for the surrounding fertile farmland. In spite of this, each town needed to be captured and held for future Aryan landowners.

As the young soldier stood in front of the house, his commander began to bark orders to his platoon. "You there, check this house," he pointed. "You there, check that house," he ordered to someone else. Then the commander turned to our young soldier with the handkerchief, "You, go check the cellar behind this house! Report back what you see," he demanded.

The young soldier immediately straightened up and began moving swiftly around the house. When he reached the back, he soon found the entrance to an old cellar. He turned the brown, rusty latch and opened the rickety wooden doors, which creaked from the rusty hinges as he lifted it. Then he carefully descended the wooden steps into the cellar with his Gewehr 41 rifle leading the way. The old wooden rungs bent and creaked from his weight with each step.

When he reached the floor, it was musty and dark inside the cellar, and he kept his rifle pointed forward as he waited for his eyes to adjust. Then he began to creep through the cellar headed for the back, scanning with his rifle and remaining prepared for the unexpected as he glanced between the shelves and benches, looking for any useful supplies.

As he crept along, he heard a faint sound, almost imperceptible, so he paused. As he stood like stone and held his breath, he listened, and he could faintly hear the sound of a woman whimpering in the dark. He smiled slightly, then he stepped as quietly as he could, making his way toward the source.

When he reached the back corner of the cellar, he noticed a lumpy canvas tarp that was stretched between the back wall and a wooden workbench. As he stared at it, he could see it subtly shaking and trembling. He reached for it slowly, then ripped it away with a swift pull—revealing a girl, probably sixteen or seventeen, hiding beneath it.

When the young soldier ripped the tarp away and looked upon her, he was struck by her beauty. It had been over a year since he had seen a beautiful woman, and he had gone his entire lifetime without seeing one as beautiful as she. But she was here, alone with him in the middle of the war.

A conflict began to brew within the young soldier. Although he was captivated by her beauty and could not take his eyes from her, he was also disgusted by her dark hair and dark eyes and the dirty Russian blood coursing through her veins. Every instinct in his body told him that he wanted her more than he had ever wanted anything, but every belief in his thoughts reminded him that she was filthy, and that her filth would contaminate him.

At that moment, he had a dark idea, and he caved to his animal instincts. He decided that he would quietly take what he wanted and capitalize on his good fortune, but he would be quick and make sure that no one from his platoon would ever find out, not that they would even care.

She's the enemy, and this is war, he rationalized. *She and her kind are a fungus upon the world—an infection and a plague—and someday soon we will cleanse it all. Her kind are the weak and we are the strong, and the strong can take anything that they want; that is the natural order.*

The young soldier knew he needed to act quickly, so he began to unzip his pants. Without hesitation, he forcefully and precipitously raped the woman as he alternated between choking her and smothering her with his hand over her mouth to cut off her screams. The woman tried to cry out and she tried to move, but the young soldier was too strong and too heavy for her to break free. There was nothing she could do to stop this assault, and her soul quietly cried out in muffled tones.

When he was finished, he zipped up his trousers and fixed his uniform to conceal his deed. Then he pulled out his military knife and held it to her neck, ready to finish things and tie up the only loose end who could ever speak of his deed. But as he looked in her eyes and saw her terror, he smiled, drunk with power and reveling in the high he felt. He thought about her future, and the evil within him he'd slowly cultivated delighted in the idea that she would have to live with this pain. He knew that she would remember his face forever, and they would always share this moment—where he was a god, wielding life and death over her at his discretion and without consequence.

"I hope you live a long life, so you can carry this memory forever—the day you met a *true* man," he whispered to her in German.

To this young soldier, raping this defenseless girl was no different than raping all of Russia, France, Poland, Africa, or England. He was not just assaulting his enemy, and the enemy of Germany; he was dominating it. Something about this idea satiated his corrupted spirit, and he could not help but smile. He decided not to kill her; but instead, simply left her there, smiling as he walked away.

He walked out of the cellar and up the old wooden stairs, then around the house, where he united with his commander and a few men from his platoon. When he was asked what he had seen, he lied and reported that the cellar had already been cleared out.

The five men began to walk up the road to reconvene with the rest of their platoon, when suddenly a plane swooped in and passed overhead through the gray fog. They had heard the plane in the distance and presumed it was one of their own, so they paid no attention as it drew near. The soldiers could only glimpse the tail of the aircraft through the haze as they looked up and had a brief moment to see that a bomb was falling toward them. They watched it as it fell, and time seemed to slow down nearly to a halt, their bodies frozen in place except for their eyes as they followed it's trajectory.

By the time their brains processed what it was, it was too late. It landed virtually at their feet and exploded, sending all five men, in the form of meat chunks, torn limbs and uniforms, flying in all directions. The young soldier, along with the four other men, were killed immediately.

The young soldier did not even have a moment to understand that he was about to die. He heard a plane and glimpsed its tail, then he saw something falling, and then there was a flash and a wave of hot pressure. There was no pain or contemplation. All he felt was a minor shake under his feet before the force of the explosion ripped through his body and scattered him.

*****

For a celestial moment, there was nothing but darkness. The young soldier was still inside one of the chunks of his body, but he had no eyes and no hands and no thoughts, just a vague awareness of still existing in the darkness.

He listened, but there was nothing but silence. He could not move, and he began to grow afraid.

Just as panic began to overwhelm him, he heard a deafening explosion like a tremendous cannon had been fired—shaking loose whatever was left of him. Just then, he felt more fear than he had ever known.

Suddenly, he realized that the cannon sound was not out in the world, but it had emanated from within him. Just as soon as he understood this, there was a flash in the darkness and an incredible whipping sensation, and he felt his spirit being ripped free from his flesh.

It reminded him of a specific memory from his childhood when he held a vacuum cleaner up to a line of ants. He recalled watching as the ants scurried along until the vortex drew too close and yanked them into the air and through the tube. He felt like one of those little ants. For several seconds, he was certain that he was a tiny speck traveling at an incomprehensible speed. Then he whipped once more as he came to an abrupt halt.

When he stopped, he found himself in a bright place and down on all fours, staring at his restored hands. He was overwhelmed with relief, and there was no more darkness.

He stood up and looked around, but he was surrounded by a warm and blinding light. It was so bright that he needed to shield his eyes from it, and for the first few seconds, he could not see anything at all. Then, as his eyes adjusted and he looked forward, he saw that inside of the light there was a towering figure, and that figure was the source of the light. He could not see the figure clearly, only its silhouette, but he could tell it was enormous and bore the shape of a person.

The young soldier slapped his chest, face and stomach with his hands. "Who are you?" he asked the figure in his disorientation.

"I Am," the voice replied.

The young soldier did not understand. "Where am I?" he asked.

"You are standing before the Lord," the voice replied.

"Why am I here?" he asked.

"Because you have died. You are here for judgement," the voice answered.

The young soldier could not comprehend the figure before him, but in his heart and bones, he understood the words spoken. He was dead and standing before God.

Suddenly, he remembered his last act upon the earth—raping a young girl, not even a grown woman—and now he was standing before the Lord, the One who had made them both.

His heart sank and his hands began to shake. He could not bring himself to even glance at God. He kept his head sunk as he looked down toward his feet. "What will become of me?" the young soldier asked.

"You have sold your soul," the voice proclaimed. "There is so little of Me left within you, that your soul cannot take one step further to enter this place."

Hearing these words, the young soldier was stricken with grief and sadness. He felt the warmth of the glowing light before him, and a peace he had never known. He never wanted to leave. "Now that I have known this place, I desire more than anything to dwell here," he said. "Is there nothing redeemable within me? Am I eternally damned?"

God looked down at the young man, and he felt pity for his lost child. "You have caused great pain—both to the innocent girl who will carry your memory forever, and to me, having to watch my child suffer so greatly at your hands. If you ever wish to step before me again, you must go back and tell the truth," the voice of the Lord proclaimed.

"The truth?" the young man asked, not understanding.

Before he received an answer, there was another great flash of light and a tremendous boom like a cannon. With a mighty snap, he was whipped through a vacuum once more and flying through the abyss until he collided with his body back on earth. Suddenly, he was staring down at the black and gray handkerchief from his mother.

He was dizzy and disoriented and on the verge of vomiting, unable to catch his breath. Then suddenly, his commanding officer barked at him, snapping him out of his trance. "You there, go check the cellar behind the house. Report back what you see!" the commander demanded.

When the young soldier did not immediately answer, his commander was furious and began to snap his fingers. "Go check the cellar, you fool. That's an order!" he yelled in obvious frustration.

At that moment, the young soldier realized that it was not a dream or hallucination. He was being given a second chance. *But to do what?* he wondered.

He recalled his conversation with God, but he could not understand it. He put his head down in contemplation as he walked behind the house and slowly opened the cellar doors before stepping back inside. Once more, he walked quietly down the creaky stairs and then through the dark cellar, where he heard the same whimpering sounds coming from the back. Unsure what he was supposed to do, he tiptoed toward the sound with his rifle drawn and pointing forward.

When he reached the back, he saw the same lumpy tarp in the corner where the young girl had been hiding previously. He slowly lifted it away, but unexpectedly, he saw that not only was the young girl there, but an older woman was hiding with her. The young soldier was baffled, and he reflexively pointed his rifle toward them.

He studied their faces, and quickly realized that they were even more afraid than he was. He lowered his weapon slightly.

As he looked between the two women, he noted that they had similar features and hair, and a clear resemblance. He noted how the older woman was clutching at the young girl and not only comforting her, but somewhat shielding her. He deduced that they were a mother and daughter pair.

Was the mother here before and I just didn't see her? Did she witness what I did to her daughter? He wondered in horror and guilt as he looked upon them.

The two women held each other tightly and whimpered as they looked up at the battle-hardened and dirty young soldier.

What now? he wondered. "What is the *truth*?" he said aloud as he looked up.

The young soldier, not knowing what to do, left the cellar and walked around the house to his commander. When he reached him, he pointed to the house and stated, "There are two women hiding in the back corner of the cellar."

The commander raised and waved one arm, calling over two other soldiers from nearby. He ordered them to go retrieve the women, and our young soldier walked with them to the back of the house. Together, the three went down into the cellar and came out with the two women a few moments later. Then, at the orders of the commander, the women were forced to walk around to the front of the house. They clutched at one another tightly as they walked.

Our young soldier began to follow, but his body froze, and he stopped.

Remembering the airplane strike that killed him the last time, he remained in the back of the house, afraid to die once more. He listened closely for the sound of propellers, but he heard nothing. *I've told the truth, just as I was asked to. Perhaps God is happy,* he nervously thought.

As he stood behind the house listening to the sky and wondering about God, he heard the crack of a gunshot, followed by the sound of the older woman screaming in horror. Her screams pierced through him into his bones, and he felt like his heart skipped several beats.

Then he heard his commander yell something, and the crack of another gunshot rang out. Then the screams were gone.

There was deathly silence all about him, as if the entire world stood still in that moment. Life itself seemed to have been extinguished. But there was no peace in the silence, only an emptiness and a cold feeling.

The young man began to pant heavily, and he felt his head grow light. He fell down to his hands and knees, and he stared at the grass. His vision began closing in as if a dark tunnel was surrounding him and swallowing him. He felt a cold chill run up and down his body, but he was sweating across his skin like a man delirious with fever. The air left his lungs and panic set in as he desperately needed a breath but could not control his lungs to take one.

He stared down at his hands and focused his attention on the small blades of grass pushing through from between his fingers. They were painted black with blotches of soot but still they climbed upward, desperately searching for a glimpse of the distant sun that had vanished in the hazy cloud of death and ash. The dark tunnel continued to close in all around him like a giant serpent as it constricted around his body and took the last of his air. He could not control his body to stop it. Suddenly, he vomited violently and felt like he was choking on the fluid as he desperately tried to inhale but had no control.

When his stomach was empty and the grass was soaked, he surrendered to it and felt somewhat better. He could not see, but he wiped the tears from his eyes and took a breath. It was the most comforting pocket of air he had ever inhaled, like the first breath a child takes when they enter the world. He took another breath, and his body began to settle and relax slightly.

Just as soon as he felt the warm breath of peace, a hot bullet passed through his neck. It felt like he was impaled by a sword covered in burning gasoline. All he heard was a sharp whizz, then a moment later, after the impact, the sharp crack of the gunshot caught up to the bullet it was chasing. A small wisp of smoke curled out of the holes in each side of his neck, followed by gouts of arterial blood, and he fell over dead in the grass.

A distant Russian sniper, having heard the two gunshots, spotted our young soldier kneeling in the backyard and shot him from three hundred yards away. It was a perfect shot. The young man never saw the shooter, and by the time he understood what had happened, he was gone once more.

He laid on his back by that cellar door, with his lifeless eyes vaguely staring up at that confining prison of shallow gray sky with no sun and no stars—a firmament made by man and war.

*****

The moment he died, he heard the same cannon shot, followed by the incredible whipping sensation like he was being sucked through a vortex and traveling to a place incomprehensibly far away, yet close.

When he came to a stop, he was once more looking down at his hands in a place of blinding light. When his eyes adjusted and he knew where he was, he stood up and immediately began to plead with God.

"This time was different," the young soldier cried out, "there were two women and no airplanes."

"Yes," the Lord replied. "And now, instead of raping one woman, you have killed two."

"But I didn't kill them!" the young soldier begged. "I told the truth, just as *you* demanded. I followed my orders."

"Whose orders were those?" the Lord asked.

"I was obedient; I did as I was instructed; I told the truth. There were two women, and I told the truth about them," the young man continued to plead.

"Of what truth do you speak?" The Lord asked. "All people are my children, and they are equal before me. Do you believe some are worth more to me than others? Do you believe I made the world just for you—for you to take and destroy as you please?"

"What was I to do? If I had betrayed my orders, I could have been imprisoned or executed for it," the young soldier argued.

"Have I not already killed you twice? Do I not seem able to recall you at any time I choose?" God asked. "This life you know now is but a drop in the ocean compared to what I would have for you, my son. I have known you since before you were born, and I have walked beside you each day of your life. I have whispered to you on your worst days and rejoiced with you on your best. I have always known all the different men you *might* become, and I have done all I can for you while quietly honoring the free will that is your birthright."

Hearing God's Word, the young man relented and softened. "What must I do?" he asked.

"You must decide whether you care more for your life or your soul," God replied.

The young man conceded. He understood that there was so much he did not know. He understood that it was both futile and foolish to do anything but listen. "My Lord, what must I do to save my future?" he asked.

"I have given you the innate gifts of reason and intuition. I have given you truth, beauty and this world that I love. I have given you My Holy Spirit, so that you may feel as I feel and love as I love when you look upon your own children, and *know* right from wrong within the pit of your gut as your heart sinks and your breath escapes you. If humanity cannot learn to use these gifts to guide your souls, then the whole world will perish. *This* is My promise," God proclaimed.

"My Lord, please; I understand none of this," the young man pleaded desperately.

"Close your eyes so that you may see," the Lord replied. "Lower yourself to the ground in humility and put your ear to the dirt; then you may finally hear My whisper."

"Please Lord, do not make me leave this place," the young man begged as he dropped back down to his hands and knees. "I will do anything to stay."

Before he could hear God's reply, he saw a great flash and heard the boom of a cannon once more, then he was being hurled through the abyss.

*****

When he arrived through the aether, he was standing in front of that same house and staring down at his mother's soiled handkerchief.

"You there! Go check the cellar behind the house. Report back anything that you find," the commander barked as he pointed.

The young man, still unsure what he needed to do, walked behind the house for a third time. When he arrived, he stood in front of the cellar but did not reach for the latches.

Not understanding the Lord's declarations or having a plan, he intended to not go into the cellar at all, but to stall for a time, then claim he had searched it when asked.

He stood at the doors, looking to the left and right nervously as he watched for other men from his platoon who may accuse him of defying orders or cowardice. He listened for airplanes and looked to distant buildings and hills for snipers and enemy soldiers. But there was no one to be seen.

As he waited and anxiously peered around, he checked his army-issued wristwatch and wiped his sweaty palms onto his trousers. Feeling that a sufficient amount of time had passed, he took one step to leave the spot, but suddenly, another soldier came around from the side of the house and startled him.

He had never seen this soldier before, but he was wearing the signature black uniform of an SS (Schutzstaffel)

officer, with the red stripe and swastika around his left arm.
As the officer approached, the young man noted that the
officer's uniform was immaculate, as if he had just arrived in
Russia and had a brand-new uniform waiting. His suit was
perfectly tailored, and his jacket was adorned with various
medals, decorations, and insignia.

Who is this officer? the young man wondered,
knowing he had not traveled with their platoon.

As the officer drew closer, the young man whispered,
"*Standartenführer,*" under his shaking breath when he
recognized that the officer was not only a decorated officer,
but a colonel of the Waffen-SS.

The officer walked directly up to the young man as if
he had been expecting to find him there. His steps were
smooth, and his expression was light, almost smiling, as he
approached.

The young man was in awe of the officer as he
studied him. The officer was tall and slender but broad in his
shoulders and athletic of build. He had light hair and piercing
blue eyes. He walked with a posture similar to that of the
finest thoroughbred horses: proud, tall, and very strong. His
steps were swift and silent, but powerful like the steps of a
lion.

As the officer drew within a few feet, he smiled to
the young man, revealing his perfectly-fitting teeth that were
as white as new snow. In that moment, the young man had
the thought that he had never seen a man as handsome or
physically gifted, almost impossibly so.

When the officer was right in front of him, the young
soldier snapped to attention and corrected his posture so as to
not arouse any suspicion, eschewing a salute because they
were in an active combat zone.

The officer nodded back smartly as a substitute for a
return salute, then addressed him, "How goes it brother?" he
asked.

"Sir, very well," the young soldier replied nervously.

"What are you doing right here?" the officer asked.

"I was ordered to check this cellar," he replied.

"And?" the officer questioned.

"It's empty, sir," he said with a subtle tremble in each word.

The officer studied the young man and looked him up and down, but somehow, he did not seem convinced. "Is it now?" he asked.

As the officer stared, there was a deathly silence, and the young man could not meet the officer's gaze. He felt a bead of sweat slowly rolling down his forehead, and he tried not to fidget, but he nervously wiped it away as soon as it reached his brow.

"I will ask you once more, what is in the cellar?" the officer calmly repeated.

Just then, the young man felt confused, almost disoriented, like he was dreaming. There was something disturbingly familiar about the officer, but he could not explain it. He was certain he had never seen or met him; but somehow, he sensed that he knew him.

The officer stared at the young man, awaiting a reply.

"It's empty, sir," the young soldier timidly answered.

"Check it again," the officer said.

"I was just…" the young soldier began but was quickly cut off.

"I said, check it again," the officer tranquilly insisted.

Then, as the officer stared at the young soldier, his face began to shift. Suddenly, he was smiling from ear to ear. The young soldier, who was previously afraid, was now horrified. The smile of the officer was not friendly or endearing, but predatory, as if he knew something the young soldier did not. His face reminded the young soldier of the smile upon a cat's face when it catches a mouse and toys with it for hours, refusing to kill it or let it escape because that would end the game. The officer's eyes blazed with delight, as if they were in the early stages of a similar game.

At that moment, a thought struck the young man that made his blood run cold. For a moment, he was certain that he was staring in the eyes of the Devil himself. Even worse, the Devil was staring back at him, toying with him in a contest from which there was no escape.

"Check it again," the officer repeated quietly, continuing to smile and never breaking eye contact or blinking.

The young man slowly turned and opened the cellar doors, then cautiously walked down the creaking wooden stairs before tiptoeing through the cellar. When he reached the back, he pulled away the tarp once more and saw the same girl and her mother, just as he had seen the last time. The two women were curled up in a ball, clutching one another desperately. They were very afraid, but so was he.

It never even occurred to him to point his rifle at them.

His own sense of terror tempted him to drag the women upstairs to appease the Devil. He felt a heavy and impending sense of doom at the thought of facing him once more and being on the receiving end of that wicked smile and relentless stare. His hands trembled slightly as he continued to clutch the tarp.

But then he thought of coming before God once more and knowing he had failed for a third time. As much as he feared the Devil, he was even more frightened of the One who came before. He wrestled with this thought for several seconds before improvising a plan.

The young man quietly began to lean in toward the two women. As he did, they shrieked slightly, and their whimpers grew more severe. Instead of grabbing them, the young man put one finger to his lips and gestured for them to be silent.

Despite the language barrier, the mother understood. She put her hand over her daughter's mouth to conceal her sobs. Then she placed her other hand on her daughter's hair and tucked her head into her breast to comfort her.

When this was done, he whispered to them with the small bit of broken Russian he could speak, and he tried to tell them he was a friend and to be silent. He sincerely hoped they understood.

Then the young man took the tarp and slowly pulled it over the women to conceal them once more.

This third time, somehow, he saw them differently. They were no longer strangers, and they certainly were not his enemies or vermin. They were very much like his own mother and sister—beautiful, sacred, and worth his life to protect. He did not even recognize this shift in his spirit as it was happening; he only knew that he needed to save them if he could.

After covering them up, he left the cellar in a hurry and emerged into the open air behind the house. When he came up, the colonel was standing nearby with two other soldiers. He turned his gaze toward the young man and watched him closely as he emerged emptyhanded.

"Well?" the colonel asked. "Did you find anything of interest?"

"No," the young man replied. "It's empty."

"Shame," the colonel said dismissively, "I thought perhaps you might find something for our men to eat. They have been moving for many days and nights. Do you see how hungry they are?"

"Yes," the young man answered as he visibly began to sweat. "Perhaps the next town will have more; this one packed everything and fled before we arrived."

Just then, the colonel's smile reappeared as it slowly spread across his face and the corners of his lips stretched toward his ears. Once more, it was like he knew something that the young man did not—some cruel joke where our young man was the helpless punchline.

The colonel stared at him so fixedly with his piercing blue eyes that the young man wondered if the colonel could see right into him and study his organs—his rolling stomach that wanted to empty itself, his quivering lungs that trembled with each breath, and his racing heart that beat so forcefully that he wondered in terror if the colonel could hear it. The young man could hear almost nothing else.

Then the colonel broke his gaze as he turned his head and gestured for the two other soldiers. "Comrades, go and check this cellar. Perhaps you will find something that our comrade has missed. Go now and be thorough," he ordered.

"But it's empty," the young man said as he took one step toward the cellar. But the colonel held up one hand, halting the young man.

The two other soldiers disappeared down the cellar stairs, creaking as they went, and the world was quiet once more.

As he waited, a bead of sweat rolled down his nose. Through the silence, he could swear he heard it hit the grass beneath his feet when it fell. The colonel never stopped staring at the young man, his cold eyes boring into him, and his wicked smile never faded.

He knows, the young man's thoughts raced in horror, *I don't know how, but he does. He's the Devil; he has to be. He's loving every moment of this. I'm the rabbit, and he's the lion. He has me, and we both know it. He never blinks. Please God make him blink; show me that he's only a man.*

Suddenly, the sound of the creaking stairs cut through the silence, and two slate-gray helmets slowly emerged from the cellar. To the dismay of our young man, the two soldiers were grunting and laughing as they dragged the two women out with them.

As the two women emerged, they kicked and screamed; pleading for mercy in their Russian tongue as they were dragged into the gray daylight and pushed down into the ashy grass.

The soot in the yard immediately stained their dresses and reminded the young man of the handkerchief in his pocket. His heart pounded so forcefully as he watched that he felt as if his ribs might break open from the inside. He felt a sensation like his heart, liver, and lungs had fallen through his guts and left him empty. But he was frozen in place, unable to run or fight—just a pair of eyes witnessing true evil, like he was a spectator watching a horrendous film.

While all this was happening, the colonel never looked away. He continued to stare at the young man and smile.

"What an excellent discovery," the colonel said in a casual tone when he finally diverted his gaze. "I had a feeling there was something to eat in the cellar. Gentlemen, take the women around to the front of the house. Let's have some fun, shall we?"

The two soldiers proceeded to drag the women by their hair through the grass as they inched their way around to the front.

The women never stopped trying to fight and claw at their assailants. They swore and kicked and did all they could, but more soldiers came over to help drag them. Their struggle for freedom was futile, but they never stopped trying.

"Come and see, comrade. I insist," the colonel said as he draped his arm around the young man's shoulders and nudged him until the pair began following the mob.

When the women were dragged to the front, they were thrown upon the ground in the middle of the road. Soldiers gathered around, hesitating, in that no one knew what would happen next. The small crowd fixated upon the two beautiful women, and the looks on their faces was palpable, almost drooling like starving dogs eagerly watching their master prepare them a meal.

When the young man reached the mob, he was horrified by their hungry and relentless stares. As he watched, it occurred to him that although every individual is capable of being seduced by evil and committing great evil, a group of men seduced by it has no limits—no line they will not cross or moment of sobriety where they might turn back. When a whole group falls prey to evil, their spirits freefall into Hell and their bodies replicate it on earth.

And I am no different, he thought.

He thought about how only a year before this moment, most of the men standing before him were just boys—young men from throughout Germany who were inexperienced and kind, fresh out of school and naïve to much of the world, innocent of all crimes. A year ago, they were just boys who wanted to view themselves as noble and heroic and brave, wanting only to earn honor and make their families and country proud. A year ago, when they first joined the war, they did not even question whether they were the heroes serving on the heroic side of it—the answer seeming so obvious that it never warranted the question. *What has happened to all of us? When did this happen to all of us?* he wondered.

The anticipation continued to build amongst the soldiers, and they slowly began to lean in as they crept forward, inching their way closer and enclosing the women as each man wanted to be first. Hunger, hatred, lust and joy flowed through their veins like liquid fire. Each man in the mob knew what they were about to do and what everyone else would do; the only question was when they would have their turn or when they would stop.

Then the officer slowly pushed through the crowd until he was standing over the two women. "Gentlemen, an unexpected bonus. The Fuhrer thanks you all for your service and commitment to the cause of *Truth*," he told them with his evil grin as he cheerfully looked to each man.

"Truth?" the young man repeated to himself, struck when he heard it.

At that moment, he realized that the unsettlingly familiar characteristic of the officer was not his face nor his figure but his voice. *His voice is nearly identical to the voice of God,* the young man thought in a panic, *how can this be? This man can't be God. I'm certain that he isn't. But it's so hard to tell. His voice sounds like a recording of God or a mild distortion of His voice through a radio.*

The officer continued, "You see? War is not all bad," he declared with a smile as he pointed to the women. "Enjoy this, my gift to you. There's plenty to go around, and we're in no rush. Take all the time you need."

The soldiers, who more than ever resembled deprived dogs, continued to lean in closer as they suspiciously glanced to the left and right to read the other men around them. Suddenly, one soldier leapt toward the middle, creating a frenzy in the mob. Several other men jumped forward, none wanting to be last, and men pushed from the back as they tried to reach the middle. The soldiers grabbed at the women's hair and clothes and arms with their dirty hands, ripping their dresses and tearing the fabric with their claws. Some even struck and kicked the women, both for fun and to make them submit. They delighted in their power, growing drunk from wielding authority over life and death. But the women never stopped fighting.

At that moment, as the young man watched in helpless horror, frozen in place, he heard a faint whisper within him. *Stop them,* the whisper said, but it was very quiet and sounded far away when he first heard it.

Then, the whisper grew louder. *Stop them,* it demanded.

But the young man was stricken with so much panic that he could not even control his limbs to move a single inch. The whisper slowly grew in strength, but it could not drown out the chaos and mayhem of his surroundings.

Suddenly, the whisper refused to be ignored any longer, and it exploded into a mighty roar within his head. It was so loud that he reflexively threw his hands up to cover his ears. The voice roared once more, and it was as loud as the cannon shot he heard each time he died. *"Stop them!"* the voice shouted. *"Stop them!" "Stop him!"*

In an instant and without thinking, the young man leapt into the crowd like a ferocious boar. He yelled his battle cry and swung furiously with wild punches going left and right into the mob. He hit two men, then missed the third, causing him to stumble and then fall to the ground atop the women. From the ground, he did not stop fighting, and he kicked viciously at the lot. He hit one soldier in the chest with his boots and even knocked out the two front teeth of one unlucky man who could not move his chin away quickly enough.

He roared savagely as he kicked and hit, and the other soldiers tried to grab hold of him to pull him out of the middle. Then the abrupt crack of a gunshot was heard from a few feet away, and everyone stopped. When they all looked up, the officer had his Luger pistol pointed into the air, still smoking from the discharge.

"Everyone, stop," he calmly said.

Everyone froze in their tracks and the world was silent once more. Then he walked into the crowd and gestured with his pistol for anyone in his way to scoot aside as he moved toward the middle until he was standing over our young man and the two women he was guarding behind him.

The young man looked up at the devil. Behind him, the faint sun was finally trying to break through the clouds above them. For a moment, all the young man could see was the silhouette of the Devil. It reminded him of the silhouette of God, only it was the exact opposite.

"You are not the light," the young man whispered.

The officer looked down with his evil smile as he cast his shadow over the young man. "See you soon," was all he said.

Then the colonel shot the young man in his right eye, and the young man's body immediately went limp—collapsing back before lying flat on the road with his arms extended. The two women screamed even harder, and the mother covered her daughter's eyes as the officer slipped his smoking Luger back into its holster.

*****

The deafening boom of another cannon shot sound rang through his consciousness as the young man was ripped through the aether once more.

When he came to a stop, he was standing before that blinding light for a third time. He put his fingertips to his eye where he had been shot, but there was no wound. He fell to his knees and began to sob uncontrollably.

"Lord God, please don't send me back there. I cannot go; I can't live this even once more. I've faced death three times today, and I cannot bear to face it a fourth. I've tried to do what you asked, but I've failed. I faced the Devil, and he beat me. I am not strong enough. I can't see or know or feel any more death and torment today; my spirit can't take it," he pleaded with God.

"I will send you back one thousand times more if I must," God replied.

"Please, Lord!" the young man cried out.

"You will go as many times as is needed," God told him.

"Needed for what?" the young man asked desperately.

"Needed for you to understand," God answered, "each time I send you, you are learning."

"Learning what?" the young man asked.

"To think for yourself; to stand in opposition to the Devil and to your country and to the entire world if you must. You must learn to use what I have given you, and you must learn the mind of your enemy so that you may resist him. You must learn how to find My voice within you," God answered. "You have a sense of *what* I am asking of you, but you do not yet understand *why* I am asking you. I am not sending you back to harm you; I am sending you back to save you and many more."

The young man was silent, aside from his quiet sobs. He thought desperately, looking for a way out, searching for the words he needed, but they would not come. God saw the agony in His child and took pity upon him.

"The last time I sent you, you did all that you could," God told him. "You faced a great evil, and you sacrificed your body to defend the gift of life. You have made Me proud, My son."

"I don't understand any of this," the young man said through his tearing eyes.

"When I created you, long before you were born, I gave you a soul; this was the gift of existence. Twenty years ago, I gave you a body upon the earth to experience the miracle of living and become real. I was there on the day of your birth, and I stood over your parents' shoulders as they stared down at you in wonder and joy and hope for everything you could become," God explained. "When I gave you a body, I also gave you a great mind, so that you could navigate the world, serve the cause of truth and beauty, and ponder your life and its meaning. But then I gave you My Holy Spirit, so that you would always have a guide within you and walking beside you throughout the path of your life. All of these were gifts and tools for you to pursue purpose, find love and participate in the miracle of creation. I did this out of My unwavering love for you, but you have abused each of these gifts and used them to serve a different master."

"I still don't understand. You put me into this life, in this context, and I am being punished for things I did not understand and the world I was born into. Surely, you must have known who I would become and seen my path before I walked it. Was my soul doomed from the moment of my birth?" the young man argued. "I just wish to go back to my life, a simple life on the farm from before the war. Send me back to my family and I will stay home; I won't volunteer to serve. I will live a quiet life and harm no one. Please Lord, I simply wish to wake from this horrid dream."

"You wish to awake from this horrid dream? You are helping to author this horrid dream. You have taken all I have made and used it in service of evil. I have given humanity love, truth, patience, beauty and the tools to triumph over evil; yet here you stand before me," God replied firmly.

"But, my Lord, how can you blame me when the voice of the Devil sounds so much like yours? How can men discern truth from evil when it is so easy to be deceived?" the young man beseeched God for answers.

"It is true. Men can be easily led astray when they stop listening for My voice within. Men fall prey to the Devil because they do not understand him. They see the glow of his morning star rising in the East and they marvel at it, mistaking the reflection he casts for the *real* light," God explained. "You must learn that the Devil would much prefer to recruit you than kill you. He celebrates every individual that he can persuade to turn away from Me. He will give you all you believe to desire, all the physical pleasures of the earth, then watch you annihilate your soul when you discover too late that most of your desires are fatal to your spirit. He will corrupt you from within, then send you into the world to assist in the corruption of others; that is his aim."

"But are you not a *just* God? You designed it this way. You created the Devil and me and this world. You stacked the deck against us. How can you condemn me to Hell for that which I did not know or understand?" the young man argued.

"I have never condemned a man for what he did not understand," God answered, "I hold all men accountable for what they *do* understand. You forget that I have known you for eons longer than you have known yourself. I was there for every moment you were tempted by corruption and evil, and I was the voice of good that you wrestled with. All men will wrestle with good and evil, and none are judged for it. But all men are judged for the times they succumbed to evil and let it guide their actions, beliefs, and speech. Heaven and Hell patiently wait outside the door of all men, both seeking a simple invitation inside. The choice of which one you invite into your life has always been yours to make."

With that, God said no more, and the young man was left contemplating. As he thought, something shifted within him. In his heart, he was no longer a German soldier. He was beginning to understand how little he knew and how much more there was to know, and his spirit reverted to that of a child.

He stood, wiping his tears upon his sleeve. He was desperate not to go back to that house and face those women or that wicked officer or another death, but he knew that he had abused his free will, and now God was forcing him to eat the crop of the seeds he had sowed.

The young man was not happy with the Lord, but he knew that God was not the cause of his pain.

A day of torment is better than an eternity of it, he realized. "Lord, I submit to your will. If this is what I must do, then I will do my best," the young man said as he dropped to one knee.

*****

With a great flash and another thunderous boom, he vanished from that heavenly place.

When he landed and regained his bearings, he found himself sitting in a wooden chair in a large room, surrounded by people. He looked around to orient himself. He was no longer in the war, but nothing was familiar. He was in a large room he had never seen and was surrounded by dozens or more people whom he had never met. He studied the room and its details to understand where he was.

This is a courtroom, he thought to himself after processing all he saw.

He looked down and realized he was wearing a suit, but he was handcuffed. In his astonishment, he looked around anxiously, bringing additional attention to himself from the dozens of people who were already watching him closely. He did not know why he was there and why he was a prisoner.

There was a man seated next to him, unhandcuffed, who, by his actions and appearance, seemed to be a lawyer. There was a sheaf of papers on the table in front of him. The young man leaned forward and studied the piece of paper at the top of the stack, and his eyes caught sight of his own name printed prominently upon the sheet. He picked it up and began to read it as quickly as he could, learning from this piece of paper that the year was 1946, and he was on trial for war crimes.

The metal handcuffs and chains chimed slightly as he reached for the papers and grabbed the entire stack. He began furiously scanning through them and reading as much as he could. He lost focus of the room and time seemed to stand still as he went through each of the pages, learning about where he was and all the crimes he was accused of—attacking civilian populations, torture and cruel treatment, murder, rape, mutilation, and participating in forced medical procedures and/or experiments.

He learned that Germany had lost the war. The once beloved Chancellor of the Reich, Adolf Hitler, had committed suicide in the final days, and many German soldiers were now standing trial for their actions during the war. The documents also indicated that after his time in Russia, he joined the Schutzstaffel (SS) and eventually became a mid-ranking officer, a Captain, stationed at Dachau—one of the first concentration camps—a place so brutal and shrouded in secrecy that even German soldiers could only whisper rumors about what took place on the other side of its stone gates—the number of people it housed, its death count, and the horrendous medical experiments being forced on the prisoners in the name of 'research'.

According to the documents before him, all the dreams he held dear when he first joined the war had come to fruition—he served bravely in Russia and returned from that front safely, graduated into the SS and quickly climbed the ranks until he was an officer—entrusted to lead men and hold national secrets. He had achieved everything he once desired—proving to the Fuhrer and his fatherland that he was a worthy son—competent, committed, and brave—a great warrior and exemplar Aryan. It was everything he envisioned becoming on the day he stood in those great lines in 1941.

Then, as he continued down the stack, he saw a photo of himself and two other soldiers, posing in front of a massive pile of bodies. The bodies were of men, women, and even small children, as thin as skeletons and piled more carelessly than sandbags. In the photo he was grinning triumphantly, as if he had achieved something.

I did these things? he thought to himself in astonishment as he looked at the photos.

After meeting God and facing His trials, it seemed impossible that he could commit such heinous acts and do it with pleasure. He knew the images were real, but he no longer knew the man in it. He knew his own face and eyes and smile, but everything else about him was foreign.

As he stared at the bodies in the photograph, he wondered about the lives they left behind and their families—people who loved them dearly and were praying for them and holding onto a precious but futile hope of them ever coming home.

Tears began to silently form and roll down the sides of his face as he stared. His handcuffs rattled faintly as he slowly went through his pockets, looking for something to wipe them away. When he checked his right trouser pocket, he found something soft and familiar folded up. As he recognized its gentle and comforting texture, he momentarily felt safe and back at home with his family. Then he pulled it out to use it.

It was the handkerchief from his mother—a cherished but distant memory of his home and a remnant of a simpler time when he was just a boy, surrounded by love and sunshine and curiously exploring a big and beautiful world of infinite possibility. He felt warm as he dabbed it to his cheeks and smelled the fabric.

He looked down to it, and it was mottled throughout with faded stains of pale gray, black, and reddish brown. Each of these stains was a story. Each stain was evidence of his time in the war and every crime he committed—all partially concealed but impossible to fully wash away.

He was heartbroken when he noticed. He recalled the day his mother gave it to him, and he wondered how he could ever look her in the eyes again if he had the chance.

Suddenly, he realized that everyone was staring at him. He paused and looked around. He did not know why everyone was watching him, until his lawyer leaned over to whisper to him.

"You have to answer the judge. Tell him *not guilty* like we discussed. You were only following orders. You were under extreme duress," the lawyer said.

The young man stood up slowly to address the court. He had too many thoughts whirling in his mind to keep them straight, but they were overshadowed by the immensely cumbersome feeling of guilt that weighed him down like his organs and limbs were filled with lead. It was the heaviest he had ever felt, and it took all his strength to remain standing. His mind raced, but all he could feel was an insurmountable tiredness that made him want to curl up in a dark hole and sleep for days or months or permanently.

He did not know what to say when he stood up. *Why am I here? What does God wish to show me?* He wondered. *What is true?*

Everyone waited anxiously for his reply, and the silence about the room was almost deafening.

Finally, he spoke, "Your Honor, for the crimes I am accused of, these awful crimes of war and genocide and evil, I plead…" then he paused.

The courtroom stared at the young man waiting, then they began to look around to one another and fidget in their seats as the seconds passed in more silence.

"I plead guilty," the young man confessed in a near-whisper without looking up.

"Pardon?" The judge asked.

The young man's lawyer immediately sprang to his feet to intercede. "Your Honor—" the lawyer tried to explain.

"I said that I plead guilty," the young man interrupted loudly. "I did these things; I did all these things. The people I did them to and their families deserve justice."

At that moment, the young man looked up at the judge, truly seeing him for the first time, and his heart sank when all he saw was the Devil himself; identical in appearance to the SS officer but adorned with the robes and gavel and accoutrements of a judge.

"So be it," the judge said with the same evil and predatory smile he had worn before. "Very well, if that is your *truth*."

Just then, an older man from the back of the courtroom sprang forward, shoving one of the police officers down to the ground as he dashed frantically to reach the front of the room. As he ran, his right hand slid into his coat pocket, drawing out a small pistol.

He ran directly up to the young man and yelled in a thick accent, "For my wife and my children, whom I will never see again!"

Then he pulled the trigger and shot our young man in the chest. The young man fell back and laid flat on the wooden courtroom floor as officers tackled the older gentleman and wrestled for the gun. There was shouting and chaos and boots pounding on the wooden floors as men scurried from here to there, but the young man could only hear it all as a distant rumble.

As he was bleeding out in the courtroom, his eyes fell upon the judge. The judge stared back at the young man smiling that familiar evil smile—never blinking, and never looking away. Then the judge whispered, "I'll see you soon."

That was the last thing the young man saw.

* * * * *

Suddenly, there was another flash, and the young man heard the cannon boom sound as he felt his body again hurling through the aether. To his surprise and confusion, when he stopped, he was not standing before God. Instead, he found himself alive on earth, but in a new place. This new place was not immediately familiar, and it was very dark and quiet and cold, with a musty odor and damp feel to the air.

He was huddled up into a ball and hiding behind a tarp with a wall behind him and to his right, and some sort of workbench or table to his left. Right away he noticed that something about him felt different. He felt smaller, thinner, and even his breathing was different. *Where am I? What's happened to me?* he wondered.

He put his warm and soft hands to his face and realized that they were not his hands, and it was not his own face that he knew moments earlier.

Then he ran his hands down his neck and then down his chest. Suddenly, he realized that he had breasts and was wearing some sort of a dress. "I'm in a woman's body," he said aloud in astonishment in a voice he did not recognize.

Then, in that dark place, there was a loud creaking sound as a hatch door swung open and a distant light began to subtly shine through. He immediately knew where he was, and his heart sank in horror.

Lord, not here. Please God, put me anywhere but here. He thought. *I'm in the cellar, and I'm the young girl hiding in the corner.*

The young man did not know what to do and there were no weapons around him. He stayed where he was, hoping not to be seen. As he sat there, curled up in a ball and shaking, he heard footsteps slowly moving his direction.

Before he could come up with any plan, there was a man standing over him and breathing heavily. The man stood still for a moment, then swiftly snatched the tarp away and threw it aside. He looked up at the man in terror, and all he saw was the barrel of a rifle pointed his way and his own familiar face staring back at him.

As he looked up at himself, he could not see the dashing young German man in the prime of his life with bright blue eyes and golden hair that he once knew. All he could see in himself was a cold, heartless, battle-hardened vulture—a locust or a savage Viking who had been marching all through Europe, pillaging and groping everything of value with his friends and all their filthy hands. As he studied his old face, all he could see was a lion delighting in his good fortune to have stumbled upon such a treat.

The soldier stood over the girl silently, and it was clear that he was contemplating what he would do next. Suddenly, an evil smile came over his old face and he began to unzip his trousers and untuck his shirt.

He looked up in horror from inside of the girl's body, as his former self leaned in and put one hand over her mouth so that she could not scream. In that moment, as he stared at his old face, he recognized in his own eyes and smile, the face of the Devil.

Is this what she saw when I first found her? he wondered in horror.

The shock of seeing the Devil in his own face was almost too much to bear. Just then, he understood; he understood all of it. For the girl, it was not a handsome young man who had crept up and found her; it was evil itself. He knew what she saw and could feel how she felt, and he contemplated how he could ever live with himself if he were to survive God's tests—how he could ever fully wash away the stains on his soul.

This is what God set out to show me. Not that the Devil is one person in one place, but that I am him. He lives out his pleasures through me. He dwells within me and many others, just waiting for his moment. He sits dormant for as long as it takes. He delights in the terror and death which I cause, and the power I feel when I cause it. My hands are his hands, and my eyes are his doors to enter the world. He owns my soul, and it is I who signed the deed over, the young man realized.

As the Devil within his former self held his dirty hand to the girl's mouth, he began to violate her. She was powerless to stop the assault, and as much as she pushed with her arms, his former self was too heavy and too strong. His warm and rotten breath was pungent in her face, and it made her nauseous. Living with his former self he had not realized how much his body smelled of death and decay.

There was nowhere she could go, and no way out. Our young man, now a woman, stared helplessly, and she endured as best she could.

The Devil in his old face never stopped staring, never stopped smiling, and he never blinked.

Please make him blink, the young woman thought.

But the Devil never does. His eyes remained fixed, elated by every microscopic detail of the terror he was inflicting, and refusing to miss even the slightest moment of it that could pass during a blink of the eye. He delighted in every flinch, every gasp and every whimper, and he wanted that single moment to last for an eternity.

Then a tear rolled down the cheek of the young woman, and the Devil leaned in and licked it. The young man in the woman's body suddenly recalled that he had done this very thing to this poor girl but forgotten, and he was ashamed and disgusted with himself. In that moment, he realized the extent of just how evil he had become.

Upon this realization, his guilt sank deeper, and he wanted to die. He wanted to be anywhere in the universe except inside this woman's body, or, even worse, inside his old body with the blood on his old hands that could never be washed off. If it was up to him, he would have preferred to cease existing altogether than to go back to his old self and live with what he had done.

Although the ordeal was only several minutes, it felt like an eternity of torment. There was no way he could have previously understood how this violation felt to the young girl. It was a form of death—the death of her innocence, the death of her hopeful optimism that most people are good. He had access to her memories, and he knew that before this assault, she was a virgin, and this would forever be her first experience with a man.

In some ways, it was crueler than death because she would live to remember it. If she survived the war, this moment would live on within her for the rest of her life. It would torment her in her waking life and in dreams. He understood, seeing the world through her eyes, that she would never forget his face. *How can she ever trust another man or ever be intimate with one?* he wondered.

Knowing what some men are capable of, it was unlikely that she would ever be close to another for the rest of her life. He knew that she would never live a normal life after this. *And who could?* he thought. *I've destroyed something beautiful—something sacred—and it can never be restored.*

With this realization, the young man in the girl's body sobbed more. He knew all that he had taken from her, and that he never deserved to see God again.

Perhaps God would forgive him if he repented, *But how can I ever forgive myself,* he wondered.

He knew that some things can never be put right.

Why is God so cruel to make me endure this? he wondered. *No, this wasn't God's doing. I built this; this creation is the product of my own hands.*

As much as this was the worst moment of the worst day he could imagine, he knew that this small taste of Hell was justice. He understood that Hell is a real place—a prison or a chamber or a work camp—and it is a place which a man can build to entrap his own soul. He was an author of Hell, and he was trapped inside the story he wrote.

When the Devil had finished, he exhaled deeply and collapsed slightly in his ecstasy. His weight upon the girl made it hard for her to breathe, and she struggled, but the Devil was too content to even notice. Finally, he pushed himself off her and she gasped for air as soon as she could.

Then the Devil in the young soldier's body pulled out his knife and held it to the girl's throat. He grinned from one ear to the other as he bathed in her terror. The girl's tears wet the blade as the Devil studied her expressions. As she grew weaker, he seemed to grow stronger.

Finally, after soaking in the moment, he pulled the blade away and put it back into its sheath. Then the Devil casually fixed his uniform and acted as if nothing happened. Then he dismissively threw the tarp back over her.

"I'll see you soon." The Devil said in a cheerful tone as she listened to the sound of his boots walking away.

When she heard the cellar doors close and knew he was gone, she pulled the tarp off of her. Then she leaned forward and vomited violently before rolling onto her side and laying on the ground.

There isn't enough water in all the oceans to make me feel clean, he thought. *When I believed I could endure no more, God has once more proven me wrong. How will I ever look upon myself again? How can I go on living with the knowledge of who I am and these memories of what I've done?*

The young girl laid down on the dirty stone floors of the cellar without hope as the vomit soaked into her dress, and the Devil's stink lingered in the air all around her. She felt paralyzed from the neck down.

She stayed there for a great while in her despair. Resolved to never move again, she planned to stay in that spot until death came from starvation or dehydration or rats, whichever should arrive sooner.

"This is a just punishment, Lord, and I understand. I no longer wish to be a part of this—a part of existence. I'm finished with the entire act," she said aloud to the empty cellar as she spoke to God.

As she lay there, broken and defeated, she began to feel a peculiar sensation that she was melting into the floor.

At first it was subtle, then she was certain her body was dissolving into a liquid goo. She could not move or resist it, but she grew very afraid. Suddenly, she could not open her eyes, and all she could see was darkness, but she could feel that she had become a puddle and was now spreading out and covering the floor of the cellar.

She had never felt any sensation like it, and it was very different from being shot or blown up. There was no cannon boom or bright light or tunnel or soaring through the vortex, just a slow dissolution.

Then her liquified body seemed to find all the cracks in the floor and it began to drip through it into a vast and empty place. As the goo drained out into nowhere, she felt the sensation that she was falling through the earth, as if the interior was made of air.

She fell for several minutes, constantly gaining speed and fully aware all the while. She was a pair of eyes plummeting through a dark abyss, surrounded by nothing by falling to somewhere.

Then suddenly, she emerged on the other side, and all the goo reconvened in a new place.

*****

He gasped for air when he landed and found himself on all fours, staring at his fingers in the dirt in the open air. He could feel the sun upon his back and the top of his head, and it felt warm. He could not recall the last time he had seen the sun.

He coughed uncontrollably for a moment, and he recognized the feel of his palm as he put it to his mouth.

These are my hands, he thought. *I'm back in my body—this disgusting and wretched vessel.*

Although he was relieved to have a body, he felt no peace being inside of his. He stayed on the ground for several seconds until a man ran up behind him.

"Let me help you up, comrade," said a voice which he did not recognize.

Then, an arm came around from behind him and scooped beneath his armpit, hoisting him up to his feet. Astonished, he looked around to see where he was, but it was not familiar at first. He was surrounded by an enormous crowd of men, all filed into perfectly straight parallel lines and facing forward. He could not see much from within the crowd.

He looked down at his hands, and it caught his attention that they were perfectly clean. This was the first time in over a year his hands were not blackened with mud and soot.

They're clean, he thought in disbelief.

He turned his hands over to inspect his palms, and he saw that they were calloused below every crease—a familiar sight—the product of years of gripping wooden handles and doing honest work. "I'm still a farmer," he said aloud in his excitement.

He looked down at his clothes and his shoes. "These are my father's clothes—the ones I was wearing before the war," he whispered.

He reached into his trouser pockets and paused when his right hand found something soft and folded and familiar. He immediately knew what it was.

He pulled it out and unfolded it to look. To his relief, the handkerchief had faded stains from all the years it had followed him and caught his sweat, but it had no stains from soot or ashes or blood or war.

He pretended to blow his nose, just to hold it to his face for comfort. He inhaled, trying to recall the smell of his home, and his mind was suddenly flooded with innumerable memories of his childhood, as if he was reliving all of it just then.

He saw memories of himself and his father working on the family car and fixing old farm equipment. He saw his sister feeding the chickens as the family dog followed her around the yard, and their mother watched from the kitchen window with a smile as she cooked old family recipes. He saw every meal the four of them ate at their family dinner table—all the laughs and stories and routines, and all the times his father made them say grace before a meal—giving thanks for another meal, another harvest, and another day together.

Then he saw a peculiar vision of his parents holding him, wrapping him in that same handkerchief on the day of his birth, back when the handkerchief was still a swaddle. In the vision, he was looking over his parents' shoulders as they stared down at their newborn son with love and wonder and hope for everything that he could become.

As he watched the memory, he glanced down between his newborn-self and his parents who were gazing upon their new baby. Just then, he realized that the memory he was replaying was God's memory—a fourth set of eyes in that room, quietly sharing in their love and hope and joy.

God was there with us that day? The young farmer wondered in astonishment. *I remember He said it, but I didn't know.*

He lowered the handkerchief as the line began to move forward. When the enormous man in front of him stepped forward several paces, the young farmer glanced over his shoulders to see what was waiting for them up ahead.

One hundred meters ahead, he could see a long dull-green tent with large tables. He stepped out of line slightly to get a better look, and he could see older officers and colonels sitting at long folding tables beneath the tent and speaking with the men at the front of each line. They were seated on the other side of the table, holding clipboards and surrounded by stacks of paper and folders.

Suddenly, he realized exactly where he was. He was back at the start of the war, or at least, the start of his time in it, and he felt foolish for not recognizing that he was standing in the same enormous lines he had stood in on the day he joined. He had been so nervous that day that his only conscious memory was recalling his desire to appear stoic and brave as he nervously waited but pretended to be like stone.

I remember this day, he thought excitedly. But then a sadness came upon him. *I remember this day. This was the day I traded in the clothes of my father for the clothes of another father.*

The line continued to slowly move forward, and he was unsure what to do, so he slowly scooted forward with it.

Why has God sent me here? he wondered but did not know the answer.

He looked around at all the men in the lines and he was stricken with grief as he looked at their faces. He knew that every man there was just doing what he believed was his duty. He knew that they were brave sons of Germany, and they loved their country. He knew that each one had honor and wanted to be a good man or a hero in the eyes of his family, country, and himself.

He knew that each man there had either volunteered or received a letter saying that his country needed him; so here they all were, standing in line to sign over their souls.

Every man here is doomed—their lives and souls are forfeit. And for every man here he will likely kill two men before he dies. Do any of them know what's coming? These brave men, my brothers, my countrymen whom I love; do any of you know who is really leading our army? he wondered.

In that moment, he understood that he loved his country. He loved the land, and he loved his friends from school and his neighbors. He loved the people of Germany, and he was proud of his heritage. He loved all of these, but he now understood that everyone he loved had been led astray. Everyone he loved had been slowly seduced by evil. He understood that his honest and hardworking neighbors had been recruited by a force they could not see and did not understand. His country was about to do something terrible, and he saw no way to stop it.

He understood that this hypnosis had not happened overnight. Everyone within the country was either actively assisting the effort or simply remaining silent. Somehow, the German people now perceived their leader as being a replacement for God.

But he is not God. The Fuhrer is just a man, no more than a pawn or puppet in the larger game of another, a game which he himself cannot see, the young farmer thought.

The young farmer checked his pockets and found the draft letter which he had received the prior month. He read the letter once more and it caught his attention that the only exemption from the military draft was if he were a priest or studying to join the clergy. He instantly recognized the tremendous irony. God put him back in this line, and only a life dedicated to God could exempt him from service.

If I served God, then I would be exempt from serving the Devil, he thought. *Perhaps a man truly cannot serve two masters.*

He almost wanted to laugh at this irony when he realized it, but his spirit was too diminished by recent events to even smile. He was not sure whether to laugh hysterically, weep uncontrollably, fall to his knees and beg the Lord, or to steal the nearest pistol and shoot himself.

Instead of any of these, he quietly stood in line. He took deep breaths in through his nose and out through his mouth as he tried to control his nerves. The men around him turned to look at the strange man breathing heavily and appearing to be on the verge of a psychotic break. As they watched him, they simply assumed he was afraid of going to war, and that he had succumbed to cowardice.

The line was long, and it moved slowly. Thousands of men stood in the lines, waiting patiently with their heads held high; proud of their country and ready to die for the fatherland. This provided the young farmer a number of minutes to wrestle with God in his thoughts. As he inched his way forward, somewhere, deep within him, he began to faintly hear the Holy Spirit whispering to him once more.

Stop them, stop them, it gently nudged him.

This was the same message he had heard before; only this time, he did not know who he was supposed to stop.

"Stop who?" he whispered to himself.

The whisper of the Holy Spirit lingered in the background as he continued to think. *I can't. I can't go back,* he thought, *I will not go back. No matter what, I won't go. They can't make me go. Even if they threaten to shoot me, some things are worse than death.*

Back and forth his mind urged him to get out of the line and run for the forest in the distance. His thoughts relentlessly nagged at him; *I cannot go. They can't make me go. No matter what, I won't go. They can do anything they want to me.*

Then the Holy Spirit grew a few decibels louder in his conscience. *Stop them,* it continued to urge him on a relentless loop.

His own thoughts grew louder as they tried to focus and overcome the sound of the great lines and the voice of the Holy Spirit. But the Spirit refused to be silent, and it grew louder within him, refusing to be ignored.

Eventually, the two voices in his head completely drowned out all the noise of the great lines—the quiet conversations all around him, men coughing and sniffing and breathing, and the sound of thousands of shifting boots in the dirt. He could hear nothing else but the two voices within, one nagging him to run and the other nagging him to fight this madness.

The cacophony in his head grew louder and louder until he felt the need to look around and confirm no one else could hear it. He looked to the left and right and back behind himself, but all he saw were young men who were irritated by his staring and his erratic behavior.

When he finally reached the front of the line, the two voices were all but screaming. He walked up to the table and found himself standing in front of an old German major. The old major was short and pudgy with large glasses that made his eyes look enormous, and small red dots on his chin and neck where he had nicked himself shaving that morning. The major looked up from his clipboard at the anxious young farmer. "Name?" he asked, but the young farmer could barely hear him over the roar.

The young farmer looked down, still unsure what to do, and he did not answer.

"I'm speaking to you. What's your name?" the major demanded, growing impatient.

The young farmer read the major's lips as he spoke, but once more, he did not answer him.

"Are you deaf? If you don't answer me, I have the authority to imprison you, or worse," he threatened. "The draft is the law. You are required as a citizen of Germany to serve. If you do not, you will be considered a coward and a traitor."

Still, the young farmer did not speak. The voices in his head screamed and nagged him relentlessly—never giving him a moment of peace.

The major looked around and began to stand up, prepared to call over several men to arrest the young farmer.

Finally, our farmer composed himself just enough to whisper four words, "I will not fight," he said.

"Pardon?" the major demanded.

The young farmer spoke a few decibels louder, "I will not go," he said. "I will not fight."

"Speak up, young man," the major demanded, leaning forward with his head cocked to one side so as to listen more closely.

Suddenly, something snapped within the young farmer, and he began to savagely roar in the face of the major, causing a look of horror and incipient fear to come over the old man's face. The reflex of the old man to escape made him lurch back, tripping over his chair and clumsily falling backward into the dirt with a thud. Everyone in the lines froze as they looked to the screaming man and the pudgy major who was flailing in the dirt like a turtle stuck on its back.

After the young farmer finished screaming and terrifying the old soldier, he turned and yelled out to the enormous lines of men behind him. He yelled so loudly that they fell silent everywhere, and even the men in the back of the enormous lines could hear his words.

"You are all slaves!" he yelled. "The Fuhrer and the Devil have led you all astray. We are not on the right side of this war. There is a God, and every man here is about to sell his soul. Every man here is about to book a one-way ticket to death and damnation. Evil has led us into this war, and we will not prevail. Every man here will die as a criminal, if he isn't lucky enough to die in battle and avoid having to live with his deeds!"

He roared at the crowd viciously like a wounded bear, and soldiers came running from all directions.

The young farmer continued to shout and repeat points from this same message. "I will not fight. My soul is worth more than Germany. My soul is worth more than the Fuhrer and his ambitions!" he yelled out. "My soul is far too valuable, and the Fuhrer cannot have it!"

Men in the crowd looked to one another, and they were afraid. Many assumed the young man was insane, but some heard his words and knew in their hearts that he spoke truth. Some men in the crowd felt a sinking feeling in their organs and a cold chill, with the hairs standing upright upon the nape of their necks.

The most morally corrupt of the men simply laughed, welcoming the prospect of causing death and reaching Hell. These ones had already sold their souls, and they smiled devilish smiles as they listened.

For the men who were shaken, what they had believed was their duty as citizens now felt like a death sentence. They nervously looked around, trying to intuit how the other men felt and ascertain whether they were alone in their doubts and fears.

Hardened soldiers swiftly surrounded the young man. They unslung their rifles and drew their pistols, ready to shoot him down where he stood. But the young farmer dropped to his knees then sprawled himself flat on the ground with his face in the dirt, signaling his surrender.

The soldiers could have shot him where he lay, but for reasons unknown, they stayed their hand. This outburst was a clear act of treason and executing the young farmer at that moment would have been justified and even encouraged. But the soldiers did not shoot.

The soldiers barked at him not to move, but as they went to handcuff the young farmer, to their amazement, other men in the crowd began to get down onto the ground and put their faces in the dirt.

Soldiers, and the men who were soon to be soldiers, looked around in astonishment as twelve other men laid themselves down and chose prison or execution over enlistment.

In all, including the young man, there were thirteen men in this crowd who refused to join the war. All of them put their faces in the dirt, leaving the crowd of thousands of men entirely dumbfounded.

While none of the men were shot that day, all thirteen were taken into custody and stripped of their possessions before being imprisoned for treason, desertion and conspiracy.

*****

Weeks later, our young farmer was sitting alone in his prison cell, and the entire world was quiet to him.

The brutal guards had removed his bed and forced him to sleep on the cracked concrete floor, but he did not protest their inhumane treatment. He dealt with his lot and slept on that cement floor for months with the rodents, the bugs and only a rusty bucket for his toilet.

Throughout his time in prison, he never complained of his situation. Instead, he passed the time by simply staring up at the ceiling at the one dim and flickering lightbulb, itself imprisoned in its own rusty cage but still fighting—doing its part to push back the encroaching darkness.

Since being put in that cell, he had developed a cough, and his health was rapidly declining. He had no expectation of any medical care, and of course no one came to treat him. His only visitors were the guards who would administer a daily beating of almost clinical precision, then feed him nearly-spoiled scraps afterward. Other than that, his illness was ignored, and he fared no better, perhaps worse, than the rats and bugs sharing his cell.

In spite of all this, he was at peace.

He could not help but feel blessed to no longer see the Devil's face, in others or in himself, and to know he will never meet that young girl hiding in that cellar in Russia. If he never saw the face of either one again, he knew he would live or die as a happy man.

He knew that he could endure and even accept the external torture and pain and even death that he faced each day, so long as he was nevermore on the performing end of such atrocities.

From the inside of his prison cell, he knew he could not harm anyone. He could not rape, kill, maim, steal, or lie; he was outside of the war, outside of society, and the only thing left to do was to stare at the ceiling and to pray.

One day, as he was staring up at the ceiling, he heard the whisper of God coming from within him. "My son, I am proud of you," God said.

"My God, why do you whisper? You feel so far away," the young prisoner asked.

"I whisper not because I am far, but because I am close," God answered.

"How long am I to be a prisoner?" he asked God.

"You are not a prisoner," God answered. "Though men have confined you to a cage, your soul and your mind remain free."

"How long will I be trapped in this cell?" he asked the Lord.

"This life is but a blink of the eye within My eternity," God began, "but you will not spend the remainder of your life here. Be patient, My son. Have faith in Me, as I have faith in you."

Hearing this, our young man was comforted. Then he pondered for a moment, and there was a question he wished to ask of the Lord.

"What is troubling you, My son?" God asked.

"When I was in the girl's body, and I saw myself, I saw the Devil in myself. Is he still in there?" the young man asked.

"The Devil will always be right outside your door, ready to step through whenever you are weak," God answered. "But I will be by your side. The Devil and I are both fighting for your eternal soul, always."

"Why did you make that vile thing? I do not understand," the young man asked.

"Because without the struggle of good and evil, there is no purpose to life; there are no choices. If you were not free to choose, then you would not in any sense be real. I will tell you this, My son, truth and evil fight for the heart of every human," God explained. "The Earth exists in a place halfway between Heaven and Hell. It is a mirror of both, and pulled by both, but it could become either. The choice is, and always will be, yours to make."

"But how can I make this choice alone? How can I stop other men from being led astray?" the young man asked.

"You have already saved other men," God answered, "You just cannot see from here what has been set in motion. Look for My voice within you, and you will not be led astray. Continue to tell the truth, and never lose faith in it."

"Please don't go. My God, please don't leave me. I don't wish to be alone," the young man pleaded.

"My son, you have not been alone for even a minute of your life," God answered, "and you never shall be."

"Will you be by my side?" the young man asked.

"I will always be by your side, and you by mine," God told him. "There will always be a place for you within My home."

*****

In the several years he was imprisoned, the young man had many more quiet conversations with God. These conversations kept his spirit inspired to continue fighting for life. Although his health was still slowly declining, his talks with God kindled the inner fire he needed to outlast his tormentors.

Many days, he did not eat because no one brought him food. Many days, he was beaten because the guards were acting under instructions, or because they were bored. Most days, he was sick from malnourishment and living among his own waste.

He would often awake in the night as rats and bugs crawled over him and bit at him as he tried to sleep. He swatted and slapped at them, scaring them off for a short time, only for them to return just as soon as he was back asleep.

Despite these horrors, the young man knew that it was worth it. He still knew in his heart he had made the correct decision.

Nearly five years after being imprisoned, the young farmer was finally set free, when he was rescued in May of 1945. His liberation came about after Hitler committed suicide, and Germany surrendered. The Third Reich had fallen, and the war was over in Europe. Soldiers from other countries were marching toward Germany, finally seeing the camps, prisons and ghettos that had been built and concealed in Germany, Austria, Poland and elsewhere.

The young man will never forget that day when he heard the rapid boot steps of the German guards as they ran past the young farmer's cell. They slammed through the back door of the prison and the door crashed with a loud noise against the brick wall as they ran. Minutes later, American soldiers entered the prison and began opening up each cell, liberating the imprisoned men and women they found inside.

Before long, two American soldiers had come to the young farmer's cell and opened it. One soldier turned the key and the other pushed the cell door open, stepping inside to help the young farmer, who by then was twenty-three. When the American entered, he pulled a piece of bread from his bag and knelt down as he handed it to the young farmer.

This was the first bite of food the young farmer had eaten in three days and no food had ever tasted better. As he ate, he felt the love of God and incredible gratitude for the man who handed him the bread. He looked up at the young

American soldier and studied his brown eyes and dark curly hair.

The American soldier looked upon the young prisoner with concern as he handed him a canteen of water and inspected him for wounds and broken bones.

As the young prisoner took a much needed drink, streams of water flowed down the left and right side of his chapped lips and cheeks. Seeing this, the American soldier reached into his pocket and pulled out a white handkerchief that he handed to the young prisoner.

The young prisoner smiled and looked upward as he took it, then he looked at the chest of the soldier who had just saved him. The young American soldier had a dog tag dangling from his neck, and as the young farmer squinted to read it, he saw the name "Horwitz", a distinctly Jewish name, engraved upon it. The young prisoner could not help but be overcome with laughter, but when he opened his mouth, the sound of his weak lungs laughing was nearly imperceptible. He could not help but marvel at God's masterful sense of humor, and the ironic and humbling nature of that moment.

Just then, he knew without a doubt that God was still by his side. He knew, perhaps for the first time since his imprisonment, that he would survive the war and recover. *Perhaps the entire world will survive this war and recover,* he thought. *As much as the devil commandeers our hands to commit his evil works, perhaps God borrows them sometimes, too. Perhaps through us, God will always find a way to put things right. I just hope that we all remember what happened here, and we try to understand why it happened. Dear God, please help us to be wiser and better, so that we never have to relearn what we ought to already know.*

*****

While the young man was imprisoned, he was wholly cut off from the world and, as such, did not have access to any news, and he had no way to know the status of the war.

However, in the weeks leading up to when he was set free, he heard an increasing number of planes flying overhead and the faint sound of bombs and gunfire. He could not be certain of the reason, but he hoped and suspected that the war was being fought near the prison, which meant that German forces were being pushed back.

Though the war was no longer his business, he did sometimes wonder: *How is Germany doing? Who's winning the war? How many lives have been thrown away?* But the guards would volunteer nothing.

What he did not know was that the news of his protest, along with the twelve other men from the conscription line who laid down in the dirt, was a story which had spread throughout all of Germany.

Despite the best efforts of the Nazi leadership to censor all information about the incident, as they did with anything they wished to conceal, men were talking. Quietly, in the training centers as well as in the tents and trenches throughout the eastern and western fronts, soldiers were telling and re-telling the story of the thirteen men who laid down in the dirt and refused to fight. These thirteen men were even given the nickname, the "Dirt Disciples."

Soldiers repeated what they knew of the young man's protest speech, and many quietly wondered if what he had said was true. It took time, but eventually it could be said that nearly every German soldier had heard the story and the speech that went with it.

Men, having this story in the back of their minds, nagging at them and challenging their beliefs, began to question the war. They went into each battle with less confidence and more fear than they had held previously. Every lost battle was like throwing gasoline onto this fire. As the war turned against the Third Reich, every bit of bad news fed into and fueled this lingering doubt, which metastasized and grew like a cancer throughout the German forces.

Slowly, as more and more German soldiers began to hear rumors of their brothers committing atrocities so vile that they could scarcely be believed, men began to take seriously the claim that they truly *had* sold their souls, and they wondered whether Germany even had the moral right to win.

For the majority of men, to fight courageously in a war, they must believe they are on the right side of that war. For others, they will not fight with any real courage unless they are confident that they will actually win. When an army questions both of these at once, it cannot withstand. This was the gift of doubt set in motion by God and through our young farmer to the whole German war machine—a seemingly small act that tipped the scales of fate just enough.

It took nearly six years in total for Germany to finally surrender on May 5th, 1945, but the war was lost within the hearts of many men long before this official date.

The young farmer never realized the crucial role he had in this process. He could not see it from his prison cell, but through his hands and his speech, things had been set in motion that would impact the entire world.

As he sat alone in his dreary, dark cell, witnessing none of it and constantly wondering if he had ever done anything right, God had greater plans for the young farmer than anything he could have envisioned for himself.

*****

After his release, it took many weeks for our young farmer's body to fully recover, but he journeyed back to his home as soon as he could.

He returned to an honest, hardworking life on his family's farm—working the soil and growing precious food for his neighbors. And he was happy.

He seldom spoke of his protest or his time in prison, and he lived and died without ever describing the journey through Hell that God had sent him upon.

Although he never fully forgave himself for the memories he carried of the despicable acts he committed in his previous iterations, he honored his second chance—having gratitude for his life, only speaking true words, and having an unwavering love for his family, neighbors, and the world.

Eventually, after several years of introspection and working to forgive himself, he built the life that God had hoped for His child. He married a fine young woman he had known from before the war, and they had three beautiful children whom they raised on their small farm.

As the years passed, they grew old together—playing with their many grandchildren, laughing together at the family table over home-cooked meals, and attending their local church.

Every day, they took walks on the farm to marvel at the world's beauty through each changing season, and God always walked beside them.

Our farmer lived a simple life, but it was whole—knowing more joy and meaning than anything he had imagined for himself.

Though his contributions to history were lost in the fog of war and he was never given credit, it did not matter to him. God knew who he was, and that was more than enough.

The ripples of his good works were felt by all people, and Hell's encroachment was staved off for the time being.

The End

Thank You for Being a Reader!

I greatly appreciate the time you took to give my story a read. As an indie author, your support makes this writing dream possible.

If you have 60 seconds, hearing your honest feedback on Amazon would mean the world to me. It does wonders for the book, and I love hearing from all my readers.

I hope you have enjoyed this work, and I hope this story will leave a lasting impression!

Other Titles from G. Edward Martin
(Author's picks- Favorite Stories)

- ***The Blueberry Daughter***: A Spiritual Native American Legend and Illustrated Novella.

- ***Life in a Jar: And the Death of the Gods***
  A Greek mythology reimagining in full color.

- ***The Return Flight: A Science Fiction Novelette***
  About astronauts faced with an impossible decision.

To learn more about these titles or contact the author, please visit gedwardmartin.com

Thank you!